For native girls and boys, but also for children of all the
other races in the world, and most especially for Luna,
Pablo and Teresa
J.A.

To my mother and my daughters
G.C.

Text © 2003 by Jorge Argueta
Illustrations © 2003 by Gloria Calderón
Translation © 2003 by Elisa Amado

Groundwood Books / Douglas & McIntyre
720 Bathurst Street, Suite 500, Toronto, Ontario

Distributed in the USA by Publishers Group West
1700 Fourth Street, Berkeley, CA 94710

National Library of Canada Cataloging in Publication
Argueta, Jorge
Zipitio / by Jorge Argueta; translated by Elisa Amado; illustrated by Gloria Calderón.
Translation of: El Zipitio.
ISBN 0-88899-487-7
I. Amado, Elisa II. Calderón, Gloria III. Title.
PZ7.A73Zi 2003   j863'.64   C2003-901286-7

Library of Congress Control Number: 2003102857

Printed and bound in China

Comal: Flat earthenware placed over the fire
for cooking tortillas.
Kumquat: A small orange citrus fruit with a
sweet rind.
Guava: A small, yellow tropical fruit that
grows on trees and shrubs.
Mi'ja: My daughter. A contraction of the
Spanish word hija, meaning daughter.
Nahuatl: A language spoken by native peoples
of Mexico and Central America.
Tamales: Meat wrapped in cornmeal dough
and then steamed inside banana leaves.
Tamarind: A tropical tree.

Zipitio

Jorge Argueta

TRANSLATED BY
ELISA AMADO

ILLUSTRATED BY

Gloria Calderón

GROUNDWOOD BOOKS / DOUGLAS & McINTYRE
TORONTO VANCOUVER BERKELEY

*R*ufina Pérez was a pretty girl. Her large black eyes shone like two moons in the night of her face. When her hair blew in the wind, Rufina seemed to be dancing to the rhythm of the fields.

Rufina Pérez spoke Nahuatl and wore many-colored petticoats. All the colors of the sun were reflected in the little pearly beads she wore, as though a rainbow were shining around her neck. Her small round feet sat under the straps of her sandals like two brown tamales.

One morning when Rufina and her mother were feeding the animals on the front patio of their house, her mother said, "Rufina, now you are becoming a woman." She asked her daughter to sit beside her on the little bench in the shade of the tamarind tree.

"Rufina," continued her mother, "you have heard us talk about the Zipitio. I know that one of these mornings, when you go down to the river, you will see him. And so I have some things to tell you. Don't be afraid. The Zipitio appears to all girls who are about to become women. He can tell. And the Zipitio wants to be the very first boyfriend of every girl. He loves being in love and, besides loving us, he wants to give us advice. You will be amazed by the things he says."

Rufina listened to her mother very quietly.

"Here in the valley," her mother went on, "the Zipitio has appeared to all of us, and he has given each of us a real fright.

"It's impossible not to be scared of him because of how he looks. But when you first see him, try not to be frightened and don't run away. It's better that way because the Zipitio can be very stubborn, and it can be hard to get him to leave you in peace with his crazy notions about love. He isn't bad. He only wants to be loved because he's ugly and lonely.

"Some say that the poor thing lives on the banks of the river because he feels so sad about being the way he is.

"That's why he only comes out at dawn, so he can hide in the shadows.

"In the old days people used to say that the Zipitio was the son of a rich woman who lived around here. They said she was so rich that she buried her money in clay pots.

"But one day, bad guys heard this story and went to rob her. First they looked for the money in the house, but they couldn't find it. Then they dug holes in the patio, but it wasn't there either.

"When the woman wouldn't tell them where she kept her money, the robbers stole her little son and took him to a witch who cast an evil spell on him and turned him into a Zipitio. Ever since, he's lived along the banks of the river."

Rufina sat very still. She felt the warm breeze caress her and her mother's story wrap itself around her, though she found it all a bit frightening.

"The Zipitio," her mother went on, "looks like a child because he is small, but he is actually old. No one knows how old he really is, though some say he's even older than the stones or the river. He wears a pointy black hat with a wide brim. And he doesn't wear a shirt, so it is easy to see his shiny big belly, as smooth as the skin of a snake. But despite his tummy, when you look at him from the front, you think you are looking at his back because his feet are backward. And goodness, goodness me, his nails are as long and sharp as little knives. Now I laugh when I remember how he looks because he's going backward when he's going forward.

"Well, my sweetie," said her mother as she threw corn to the pigs, hens and ducks that were eating in the dust at their feet, "when the Zipitio appears, don't be afraid."

After that Rufina often thought about what her mother had said and, each day that she went to the river to fetch water, she wondered if he might be there.

One dawn Rufina Pérez woke up, took her jug as usual and went along the path to the river.

Everything was dark and quiet. Rufina saw how the great morning stars hung in the sky and smiled. As she walked, her skirts brushed the drops of dew that were hanging like earrings from the petals of the flowers and along the blades of grass.

When she reached the river, Rufina put the jug on the sand and walked right to the edge. She bent over to touch the water with the tips of her fingers. Wading in, she crossed herself and began to say her prayers: "Almighty God...." Then she leaned over to wash her face.

As she straightened up, Rufina could see a figure reflected in the ripples of water that trembled out in circles from where she stood.

Sitting on the rock known as Big Face was the Zipitio himself, just as her mother had described him.

Rufina froze. She was very frightened.

"Good morning, good morning, little flower. Good morning, little bunny. Good morning, Rufinita. May the fields wish you good morning. May God give you a good morning, Rufina Pérez. I am the Zipitio."

Rufina heard him say her name in his rusty voice. She felt as though hairy caterpillars were walking all over her body, and she turned and ran out of the river in great strides that made the water splash, splash, splash.

When the Zipitio saw that Rufina was about to run away he said desperately, "No, no, Rufinita, don't go. Don't be afraid. I won't hurt you. I know I'm short, and that I have a big belly, and that I'm ugly, but I'm not bad. Come back, Rufinita!"

And the Zipitio sat on the rock and cried as Rufina ran away.

Behind the hills little threads of light were dancing up to the sky, and it looked as though the sun were growing out of the earth. Rufina did not stop running until she came to her mother.

Her mother said, "Oh, mi'jita, that bandit has come out."

"It's just the way you said," sobbed Rufina.

"Of course," said her mother. "But as I told you the Zipitio is not really bad. Remember that every woman in this valley has seen him and we are all fine, even though he certainly gave each of us a big fright. Later we thought it was funny. Look at Petrona. Today she claims she was never the slightest bit afraid, although she was speechless for days after she first saw him. And La Cande says that she'd even like to see him again, although the first time she did, he gave her a fever."

They went into the house. After Rufina had changed her clothes, she sat by the fire.

"What happened to you, Mamita?" said Rufina.

"My cheeks swelled up. But don't worry, mi'ja, because all this has happened to me, too. I know exactly what to do. There's a secret…"

And with that Rufina's mother leaned over and whispered so softly that only Rufina could hear.

"You know what else?" said her mother out loud. "Right now the Zipitio is probably under the *comal*. He turns himself into flames so that he can be the one who heats your house and cooks your food.

"At night when everyone is asleep and the fire has burned down, the Zipitio eats the ashes. Then he stands in front of the house and opens his mouth wide. All the ashes he has eaten turn into little stones that fall out of his mouth. The Zipitio throws them at the roof but no one hears a thing. As the stones hit the tiles, they turn first into flowers, then into fireflies that fly off, glowing, into the bushes. Only you can hear this. And only you can hear the Zipitio's voice."

Rufina sat quietly and watched as the flames burned softly around the *comal*.

Time passed very slowly that day. The breeze carried the smells of guava, kumquat, cocoa bean and ripe mango.

Every now and then Rufina looked toward the river and thought about the three nights when her mother said she would hear the Zipitio. I hope the time passes quickly, Rufina thought. She remembered what her mother had said she should do on the morning of the fourth day.

That night Rufina's mother sat on the edge of her bed until Rufina was sound asleep. When all was still and only night animals, the wind and the stars were awake, Rufina's ears awoke and heard the Zipitio from within her deepest sleep, just as her mother had told her she would.

The next morning Rufina wasn't afraid any longer. She knew for herself that the Zipitio was not bad and that beauty doesn't only come from beauty.

At dawn on the fourth day, Rufina took a
basket and went along to the river thinking about
the secret her mother had told her. There, sitting
on Big Face, was the Zipitio.

"Good morning, angel, heart of the morning.
Good morning, Rufinita, ray of sunshine, most
precious stone. Only you know what I said last
night, how I want to protect you and love you."

The Zipitio paused and before he could go on, Rufina interrupted.

"If you love me so much I want you to prove it to me."

"Whatever you want," said the Zipitio.

"Well," said Rufina, "I've never been to the sea, but I've been told that it is as big as the sky and has salty water, whose murmurs are called waves. I want one of those waves just for me. That's why I've brought this basket, so you can take it to the sea and bring me back a wave."

When the Zipitio heard Rufina's request he was so excited that he leapt off the rock to Rufina's side and, snatching up the basket, jumped from stone to stone down the river toward the sea.

Rufina never saw the Zipitio again. But when her own daughter did, Rufina knew exactly what to tell her.